THE THREE SNOW BEARS

JAN BRETT

THE THREE SNOW BEARS

SCHOLASTIC INC.
New York Toronto London Auckland Sydney
Mexico City New Delhi Hong Kong Buenos Aires

For Katie

With thanks to the Brookfield Zoo

ISBN-13: 978-0-545-09951-6
ISBN-10: 0-545-09951-X

12 11 10 9 8 7 6 5 4 3 2 1   8 9 10 11 12 13/0

Printed in the U.S.A.   08

First Scholastic printing, September 2008

Design by Marikka Tamura
Text set in Della Robbia
The art was done in watercolors and gouache.
Airbush backgrounds by Joseph Hearne

"Come back!" Aloo-ki shouted as her huskies floated out to sea. *Oh, no!* She knew that although an ice floe is a good place to fish, it is a bad place to lose a dog team.

Not far away a snow bear family had just started to eat their breakfast. But it was way too hot for Baby Bear.

"Ow-ee!" yowled
Baby Bear. "My breakfast
burned my mouth."
"We'll go for a stroll
and let the soup cool,"
Mama Bear said.

Aloo-ki was running along looking for her dogs
when she came upon the biggest igloo she had
ever seen.

Who lives here? she wondered.

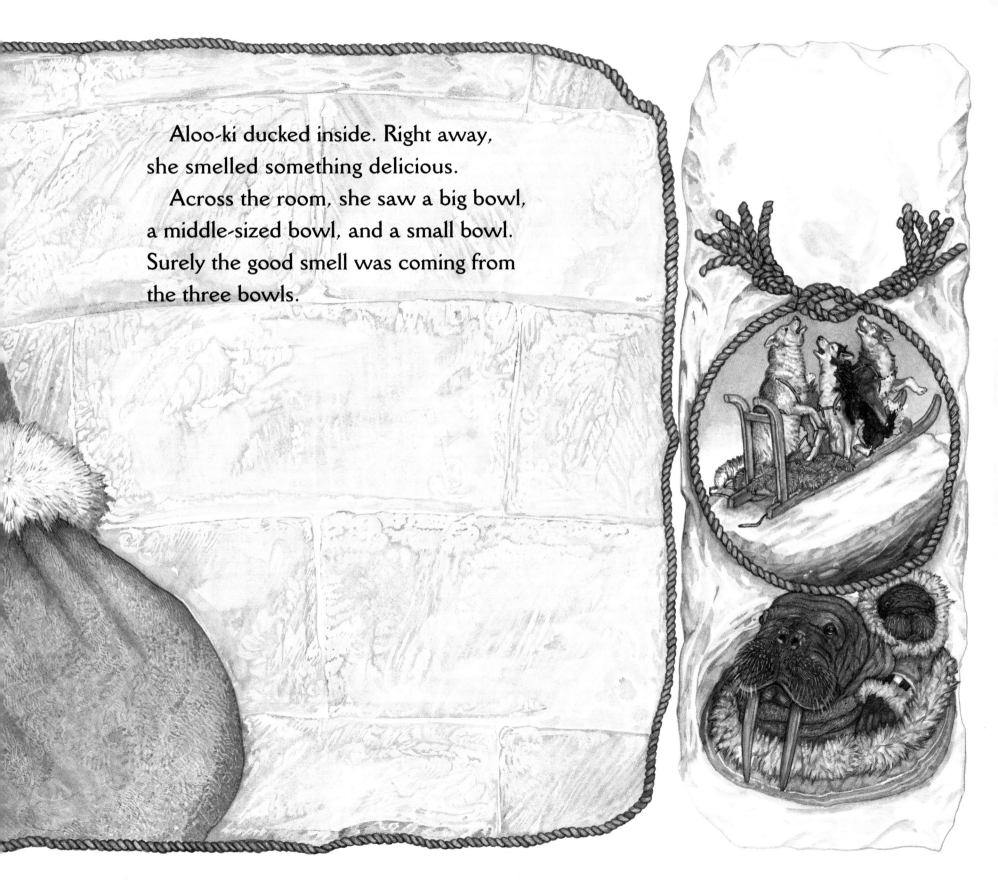

Aloo-ki ducked inside. Right away,
she smelled something delicious.

Across the room, she saw a big bowl,
a middle-sized bowl, and a small bowl.
Surely the good smell was coming from
the three bowls.

Aloo-ki took a sip from the biggest bowl.
"Owwwwww!" she cried out. "Too hot!"
She took a sip from the middle-sized bowl.
"Ewwwwww! Too cold!"
She tipped up the littlest bowl and drank every drop.
"Mmmmmm!" she said. "Not too hot and not too cold."

In the next room Aloo-ki spotted three pairs of beautiful boots standing in a row.

She put on the biggest boot. "Too big!" she said.

She put on the middle-sized boot. "Too fancy!" she said.

She put on the littlest pair. "Just right!" she said, wiggling her toes in the soft fur lining.

Aloo-ki walked into the last room and found a long sleeping bench piled high with fur covers. Heat from an oil lamp warmed her cheeks and made her sleepy. *Time for a nap,* she thought.

She crawled under the highest mound of covers. "Too lumpy," she grumbled. She tried the middle bed with the furry fringe cover, but sank down so far that she could hardly breathe. "Too soft," she said.

She rolled over into the smallest sleeping place. The furry blanket was cozy and warm and the pillow was just her size.

"Just right," Aloo-ki murmured and was asleep before she could take her boots off.

If Aloo-ki hadn't fallen fast asleep,
she might have heard her dogs
barking happily.

Papa Bear, Mama Bear, and Baby Bear
had spotted them adrift in the strong current
and gone out to save them. The snow bear
family was pushing Aloo-ki's dog team back
toward their igloo and safety.

Papa Bear crawled into the igloo and saw his big bowl sitting in a pool of spilled soup. "Someone has been tasting my soup!" he roared.

Mama Bear rushed in and saw that her soup had been sloshed around too. "Someone has been sipping my soup," she growled.

"Someone found my soup!" sputtered Baby Bear in her high, squeaky voice. "And they ate it all up!"

Papa Bear ran into the next room and saw his boots in the middle of the floor. "Someone has been trying on my boots," he boomed in his big bear voice.

Mama Bear put on her fancy boots. "Someone
has had these boots on," she huffed, "and the fur is
all bunched up."

Baby Bear saw that her boots had disappeared.
"Someone has taken my boots and left behind these
not as good ones!" she wailed.

The bears ran into
their bedroom.

"Someone has been sleeping in my bed!" Papa Bear
bellowed.

"Someone has been sleeping in my bed too!"
Mama Bear cried.

Baby Bear peeked at her little bed and squeaked,
"Someone has been sleeping in my bed, and here she is!"

Aloo-ki opened her eyes and saw
three bear noses only inches away.

She hopped out of bed and
dove between Papa Bear's
huge furry LEGS!

Quicker than a seal, Aloo-ki ran from room to room until she burst outside.

Her huskies bounced around, barking
and smiling their doggy grins.

Aloo-ki and her dogs flew over the frozen ice,
dodging ridges and cracks. She looked back
to wave a thank-you to the snow bears.

She couldn't see them, but she heard a big gruff
voice, a middle-sized voice, and a high, squeaky
voice calling to her . . .